Dionysus and the Land of Beasts

DON'T MISS THE OTHER ADVENTURES
IN THE HEROES IN TRAINING SERIES!

HEROES IN TRAINING

Dionysus and the Land of Beasts

By
Tracey West
Created by
Joan Holub and
Suzanne Williams

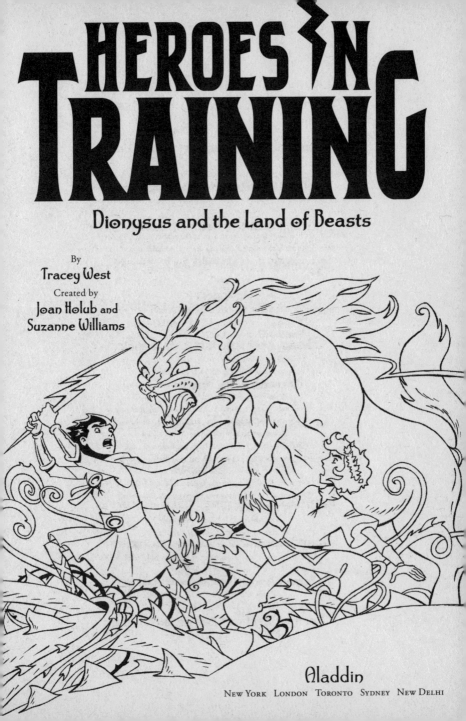

Aladdin
NEW YORK   LONDON   TORONTO   SYDNEY   NEW DELHI

ALADDIN

An imprint of Simon & Schuster Children's Publishing Division
1230 Avenue of the Americas, New York, NY 10020
First Aladdin paperback edition December 2017
Text copyright © 2017 by Joan Holub and Suzanne Williams
Illustrations copyright © 2017 by Craig Phillips
Also available in an Aladdin hardcover edition.
All rights reserved, including the right of reproduction
in whole or in part in any form.
ALADDIN and related logo are registered trademarks of Simon & Schuster, Inc.
For information about special discounts for bulk purchases,
please contact Simon & Schuster Special Sales
at 1-866-506-1949 or business@simonandschuster.com.
The Simon & Schuster Speakers Bureau can bring authors to your live event.
For more information or to book an event
contact the Simon & Schuster Speakers Bureau at 1-866-248-3049
or visit our website at www.simonspeakers.com.
Series designed by Karin Paprocki
Cover designed by Nina Simoneaux
Interior designed by Mike Rosamilia
The text of this book was set in Adobe Garamond Pro.
Manufactured in the United States of America 1117 OFF
2 4 6 8 10 9 7 5 3 1
Library of Congress Control Number 2017939226
ISBN 978-1-4814-8835-8 (hc)
ISBN 978-1-4814-8834-1 (pbk)
ISBN 978-1-4814-8836-5 (eBook)

⚡ Contents ⚡

Dionysus and the Land of Beasts

Greetings, Mortal Readers,

I am Pythia, the Oracle of Delphi, in Greece. I have the power to see the future. Hear my prophecy:

Ahead, I see dancers lurking. Wait—make that *danger* lurking. (The future can be blurry, especially when my eyeglasses are foggy.)

Anyhoo, beware! Titan giants seek to rule all of Earth's domains—oceans, mountains, forests, and the depths of the Underwear. Oops—make that *Underworld*. Led by King Cronus, they are out to destroy us all!

Yet I foresee hope. A band of rightful rulers called Olympians has begun to form. Though their size and youth are no match for the Titans, they are giant in heart, mind, and spirit. They follow their leader, Zeus, a very special boy. Zeus is destined to become king of the gods and ruler of the heavens.

If he is brave enough.

And if he and his friends work together as one. And if they can learn to use their new amazing flowers—um, amazing *powers*—in time to save the world!

CHAPTER ONE

The Search for Lost Friends

I hope the last Olympian we are looking for has awesome powers," Poseidon was saying. "Like . . . making treats appear out of nowhere."

Nine kids, each ten years old, were hiking toward a valley in the heart of Greece. They looked like normal kids taking a walk on a sunny morning, but really, they were all Olympians— gods and goddesses destined to rule the land.

"Yeah, I hope he's super strong!" agreed Hades.

"Well, I hope he is a *she*," said his sister Hera. "We could use another girl around here."

"Right," agreed her sisters, Demeter and Hestia.

"I just hope the *new* Olympian isn't a jerk," Hephaestus grumbled. The silver skull on the end of his walking stick gleamed in the sunlight.

Hermes, a boy with golden-brown hair, was the only Olympian not walking. He flew in the air next to them, powered by magic winged sandals.

"Should I take that personally?" Hermes asked. "After all, right now I'm actually the new Olympian, until we find the last one."

Hephaestus shrugged. "If the winged shoe fits . . ."

Gray-eyed Athena nudged Hephaestus. "I don't think you want to start anything, Heff."

"Are you forgetting that he loves to prank us?" Hephaestus asked.

Poseidon turned around. He had black hair, and eyes the color of a turquoise ocean. "Maybe he pranked us, but he saved us too! Hermes has mad skills! I still can't believe he turned that monster into a bunch of stars in the sky!"

Ten-year-old Zeus, the leader of the Olympians, listened to the conversation, but did not join in. The black-haired boy with serious blue eyes had too much on his mind.

It hadn't been that long ago that he had pulled a magical dagger (which he called Bolt) from a stone at the Temple of Delphi, and Pythia, who could see the future, had told him that he was an Olympian. He was a hero in training—a god destined to take down King Cronus and his evil Titans. Pythia had said that

Zeus would rule with other Olympians, too. Kids just like him.

Since then, he'd been on a crazy adventure, a quest with no rest. One by one, he'd found the other Olympians. They'd searched for magical objects that would help them defeat King Cronus and his army.

Together, they had battled Titans with awesome powers. They had faced terrifying monsters. And they'd learned secrets. Zeus had discovered that he and some of the other Olympians were the sons and daughters of King Cronus himself. They were his brothers and sisters—and family he didn't know he had.

The biggest battle hadn't happened yet, but Pythia had said it would start soon. And they needed to find one last Olympian to complete their team. But first . . .

"We can't even start looking for the last

Olympian until we find the others," Zeus spoke up. "Artemis, Ares, Aphrodite, and Apollo are still missing."

"We haven't stopped thinking about them, Zeus," said his sister Demeter. Her green eyes looked worried. "I hope that nothing bad has happened to them."

A few days ago, Pythia had told them to search for "hairy snakes." (When she was looking into the future, her glasses sometimes got fogged up, and she couldn't see things clearly.) The Olympians had split up into three groups to find the snakes. Ares, Apollo, Artemis, and Aphrodite had all headed toward the hot springs.

Zeus and his group had ended up finding the "hairy snakes"—a monster named Medusa with snakes for hair. When they'd returned to the village meeting place, they'd rejoined Hera's group. But four of their friends were still missing.

"I'm sure they're okay," Hera said. "They're probably just lost."

"You should have let me go with Aphrodite's group," Hephaestus grumbled. "*I* wouldn't have gotten lost."

"You're just jealous that Ares got to go with Aphrodite," Hera said. She shook her head, and her golden-blond hair bounced on her shoulders. "Honestly, I don't know what's so great about that girl."

Hephaestus blushed. "I'm not jealous," he mumbled.

The group came to a fork in the path. To the right was a thick forest of oak trees. To the left, a field of pale green grass. It was dotted with purple flowers that swayed in the summer breeze. In the distance, Zeus could see a low mountain.

Zeus stopped and touched the stone disc that

hung around his neck on a cord. The stone's name was Chip, and it had been given to Zeus by Pythia. Chip was one of Zeus's magical objects.

"Which way, Chip?" Zeus asked.

A green, glowing arrow appeared on the flat surface of the stone. It pointed left.

"This way!" Zeus called out, and the others followed him.

They walked for most of the morning. A few birds flew with Hermes overhead. Some insects with shiny green wings darted among the flowers. But they were the only company the Olympians had for a long time.

As the sun neared its highest point in the sky, the land sloped down. They made their way to the valley below the mountain. White smoke plumed from the top of the mountain and disappeared into the blue sky.

"Cool! It's a volcano!" Hephaestus remarked.

"That makes sense," said Athena. "Hot springs are often found at the base of a volcano."

Hades sniffed the air. "Mmm, smells like home."

For Hades, who was ruler of the Underworld, home smelled like rotten eggs and stinky socks.

"That's sulfur," Athena said, wrinkling her nose. "There are all kinds of tiny animals living at the bottom of the hot springs, and that is what makes it smell so bad. They're so tiny you can't see them with your eyes."

Hera looked suspicious. "Are you making that up?"

Athena held up her hand. A very thin string was tied around her finger—her magical object, the Thread of Cleverness.

"Stuff just pops into my head sometimes," Athena said. "I can't help it."

Poseidon held his nose as the smell got

stronger. "Gross, Bro!" he told Hades. "I can't believe you like this smell."

Hades took a deep breath. "Dee-licious!" he announced.

As they kept walking, they could see more white smoke rising from the ground. Soon they saw an almost-round pool in front of them. The smoke was rising from the blue water.

"It's beautiful," said Hestia, her brown eyes bright. As she walked, Hestia held a torch with a small, dancing flame in her hand—her magical object. If she wanted to, Hestia could create a raging fire with that little flame.

Zeus looked around. "Well, we've reached the hot springs. Chip, do you know where the others might be?" he asked his amulet.

Before Chip could point them in the right direction, a voice rang out through the foothills.

"Help us! Somebody help!"

The Olympians froze.

"Please! Someone help!" the voice cried out again.

"That sounds like Aphrodite!" Hephaestus yelled, and he ran toward the sound. He used his cane to help him move more quickly than Zeus had ever seen.

"Help! Please help!" the voice called again.

Zeus broke into a run. "Come on, everybody! Our friends are in trouble!"

CHAPTER TWO

Fooled!

As the Olympians raced toward the sound, Zeus wondered what they would find.

"Her voice is coming from in there!" Hephaestus called over his shoulder. He pointed with his staff to a cave nestled at the base of the mountain.

Zeus felt the mist from the hot springs on his skin as he ran toward the cave. Hephaestus disappeared inside it first. Zeus and the seven others raced in behind him.

After only a few steps in, they were plunged into darkness. The dim light of Hestia's torch revealed rocky cave walls all around them.

"Where are they?" Poseidon yelled.

"Shhh!" Zeus said. He listened for Aphrodite's voice again.

"Help! Help!"

"Aphrodite, we're here!" Hephaestus called out.

But after a few seconds, it was silent again.

"Something's not right," Athena said slowly. "That voice sounded like it was coming from the entrance of the cave. But we just came from there."

"Hestia, can you make your torch brighter?" Zeus asked.

"Sure," his sister replied.

The flame leaped on top of the torch, lighting

up the cave. The Olympians shrieked with fright at the sight of a creature blocking the entrance.

The monster looked almost like a horse, but its hair was bright red and it was twice the size of any normal horse. Instead of its horse head, it had the head of a large cat, with gleaming white, sharp fangs.

"A Leucrocotta," Athena whispered.

"Help! Help!" the creature said, in Aphrodite's voice. And then it started to laugh.

Hephaestus sprang forward. "What did you do to Aphrodite? Where is she?" he yelled, waving his cane. Zeus held him back.

"Hang on," Zeus said. "I think this cat-horse thing is trying to trick us."

"That's right," Athena said. "The Leucrocotta's voice can sound like any human. It tricks humans that way, and then . . . eats them."

"Clever girl," said the Leucrocotta, this time

in a deep, growling voice. "I fooled your friends, if you mean those four scrawny children I trapped the other day. I've been trying to fatten them up to make for a proper meal."

"Then they're alive?" Zeus asked.

"Yes," answered the Leucrocotta. "But they won't be alive for long. And neither will you."

Zeus let go of Hephaestus. He took the lightning bolt–shaped dagger off his belt.

"Bolt, large!" Zeus cried.

His magical object grew until it was larger than Zeus. It sizzled and zapped with electricity. But before he could hurl it at the Leucrocotta, Hephaestus let out a loud yell.

"Aaaaaaaaaaaaaaaah!"

He charged at the monster, waving his cane. Then he threw it at the beast.

The cane flipped over and over as it sailed through the air.

Whack! It smacked into the Leucrocotta, sending the creature flying backward out of the cave. The Olympians charged after the creature. Poseidon held out his trident. Hermes gripped his magical object, a wand with two gold snakes wrapped around the base, and wings on top. Hestia's torch burned brightly.

Outside, the cane flew back into Hephaestus's hand as the Leucrocotta scrambled back to its feet. Poseidon tapped his trident on the ground, and a wave of water shot out, blasting the beast.

The water carried the Leucrocotta, up, up, into the air, and then the monster came splashing down into the hot spring.

Athena ran up to the edge of the spring. She opened her cloak to reveal a silver chest plate bearing the image of the face of Medusa, the monster with snakes for hair.

"Over here!" Athena cried, and when the

Leucrocotta turned its head and looked into the shield, it froze. Its body turned into hard, gray stone, and it slowly sank into the hot, bubbling water. The monster disappeared in the spring.

"Great teamwork, everyone!" Zeus cheered.

Then the air was filled with human voices again.

"Help us!"

"Help!"

"Zeus! We're over here!"

Athena frowned. "There could be more Leucrocotta," she said.

"We'll be prepared this time," Zeus said. "Everyone, have your weapon at the ready if you have one. I'll lead the way."

Bolt sparked in Zeus's hand as he followed the sound of the voices, past the cave, and around a curve in the mountain. Hanging from a tree was a large wood cage—and inside were Aphrodite, Ares, Artemis, and Apollo!

"Aphrodite!" Hephaestus yelled.

"We're saved!" Aphrodite cried.

"Are there any more of those cat-horse monsters around?" Zeus called up.

"No!" Hades yelled back. "Just that one jerk. Is he gone?"

"Oh, he's very gone," Athena assured him.

Hermes flew up to the cage and unlocked the door.

"Let me help you down from there," he said, holding out his hand to Aphrodite.

Zeus could see Ares's red eyes flash. "Who is this guy?"

"He's Hermes, an Olympian," Zeus replied. "He can fly."

"Yeah, we can see that!" snapped Artemis.

One by one, Hermes carried the four lost Olympians down to the ground.

"So what happened?" Zeus asked.

Artemis, Ares, and Apollo seemed distracted. They were walking around, looking down at the grass. Aphrodite answered for everyone.

"When we got to the hot springs, we heard a sound like a crying baby," she explained, and Zeus couldn't help thinking that Aphrodite's own voice sounded like a sweet, bubbling fountain. She had that effect on people. "But it was really that nasty monster tricking us into his cave. Artemis shot an arrow at him but he dodged out of the way. We followed him back outside and Ares tried to attack him. . . ."

Artemis joined the conversation, holding a golden bow. "He needs to learn how to control that thing!" she complained. "The stupid spear went haywire and knocked my quiver of arrows right off my back!"

"And my lyre, too," Apollo piped up.

Aphrodite held up a golden apple. "I still had my apple, but you know it can't do much except make coins," she said. To demonstrate, she tossed the apple from one hand to the other, and a shower of gold coins fell to the ground.

"So the monster rounded us up, put us in that cage, and hoisted us up that tree," Artemis said. "I don't know how he managed with hooves for hands, but he's pretty good with a rope."

"Aha!" Ares yelled. He held up his right arm, and clenched in his fist was his magical object—the Spear of Fear. It was a powerful weapon, but Ares was still learning how to use it. "Found it!"

"Be careful with that thing!" Artemis warned.

Then Apollo walked up. He had the same sparkling blue eyes as his twin sister, Artemis, but his wavy blond hair was short, while her golden-brown hair grew down her back.

"I found your quiver and arrows, Sister," he said, holding it out to her. "Here you go."

Hera looked at Apollo. "Are you okay? You're not rhyming or singing, like you usually do."

Apollo held up two pieces of wood with strings dangling from them. "My lyre is broken, busted, gone, no longer will I burst out into song," he said sadly.

"Bummer, dude," said Poseidon.

"Was that your magical object?" Hermes asked him.

Apollo shook his head. "Not magical. Just an ordinary instrument. But we made beautiful music together."

Hermes grinned and held up his wand. "Hang on. Your beautiful music is about to get beautifuller."

"Is that even a word?" Hera asked.

But Hermes didn't lose his grin. His wand began to glow as he waved it over Apollo's lyre. . . .

CHAPTER THREE
Magic in the Air

The broken lyre floated out of Apollo's hands. The Olympians watched in surprise as the two broken pieces of wood fused back together. The strings tightened and the ends wrapped around the wood.

But the lyre kept changing. The wood pieces of the lyre transformed into shining gold. The brown strings turned into strings of shimmering silver. Then the lyre floated back into Apollo's open hands.

"Hope you like it," Hermes said. "Might need some tuning."

Apollo plucked the strings one by one. "It's perfect! Thank you, new guy."

"That's Hermes, dude," Hermes reminded him.

"That was awesome!" cheered Poseidon. "Is anyone else thinking what I'm thinking? That things would have gone much easier for us if we had found Hermes right away?"

"Yeah!" agreed Hades. "He could have taken down those Titans for us with his wand. Zap! Zap! Zap!"

"We did just fine without him," Hera pointed out. "Anyway, he didn't even try to help us with the Leucrocotta."

Hermes shrugged. "You guys had it under control."

"Hip hip hip, hip hip hooray! Our new friend Hermes has saved the day!" Apollo sang, strumming along with his new-and-improved lyre.

Zeus listened, quietly counting the members of the group to make sure everyone was there—and safe.

"Thirteen," he said out loud. "There are thirteen of us."

"I like that number," Hades said.

Demeter shivered. "I've always heard that it was unlucky."

"Well, we won't be thirteen for long," Zeus pointed out. "Pythia told us that we'll find the fourteenth Olympian soon. We have to go to the Land of Grapes."

"That sounds nice—and safe," said Artemis. "Are you sure she doesn't mean the Land of Apes?"

Zeus shook his head. "Definitely the Land of

Grapes. That much we're sure about. But I don't know how safe it will be. She said that the next Olympian we find will be the final one—and then we'll face our biggest monster ever."

Ares waved his spear. "And we'll be ready!"

Artemis pushed down the spear with her hand. "Seriously, watch that thing!"

Zeus looked up at the sky. "We've still got daylight left. Chip, which way to the Land of Grapes?"

A green arrow appeared on Chip's surface. Zeus looked at the arrow and then at the sky.

"South," Zeus said. "Come on, let's get going!"

They started walking, heading away from the mountain. As they passed the hot spring, Hades cupped his hands and took a drink.

"Mmmm," he said.

Poseidon punched his arm. "Dude, that's, like, monster soup now!"

Hades made a face. "Oh man, I forgot." Then he shrugged. "Still, it's delicious!"

They followed Chip's arrow and headed south. Hermes flew between Artemis and Aphrodite, trying to get to know the new Olympians. Artemis had a face that matched her twin brother Apollo's.

Aphrodite's long blond hair cascaded down the back of her white dress. She wore a necklace of shells from the sea—the place where the other Olympians had found her. She had bobbed toward them on a wave of bubbles, floating in a huge clam half shell.

"Hera calls me a Birdbrain. Do you think so too?" Hermes asked. The wings on his sandals fluttered as he floated upward. Then he did a perfect somersault in the air.

Aphrodite just laughed, creating bubbles that floated up around her. Ares and Hephaestus glared at Hermes.

Then Apollo strummed the lyre again.

"A monster trapped us in a tree, the monster fell, and now we're free!" he sang.

As soon as he sang the word "fell," there was a loud rumble—and then a huge *crack*!

A large tree came crashing down on the path right in front of them, barely missing Apollo! He yelped and jumped out of the way just in time.

"You ok, bro?" Zeus asked.

Apollo picked up his lyre, which he had dropped. "I think so?"

"What was that?" Hera asked.

"A wind?" Demeter guessed.

"It's not windy at all," Athena said.

Zeus looked around. There was no sign of an enemy, or anyone who could have brought the tree down on purpose.

"Must have just been an old tree," Zeus guessed. "Let's walk around it."

They followed Zeus, and Athena cast suspicious glances as they passed.

"The tree's sap is running green," she said, eyeing the broken part of the trunk. "It's not old."

"Then it was a freak of nature," Zeus said, but he did feel a little uneasy. "Let's keep going."

"Yeah, maybe we can take a food break soon," Hades suggested.

"Sure, but no monster soup," Poseidon joked.

Everyone started laughing and talking again, and the weirdness of the tree was forgotten. As they kept walking, Apollo strummed his lyre for another song.

"Our new friend Hermes is a really nice guy, he can fly so high up in the sky," Apollo sang.

As soon as Apollo finished his verse, Hermes shot up into the air like a rocket!

"Hey, what's going ooooooooooooooooon!" His

voice faded as he shot higher into the clouds.

Athena ran to Apollo. "Quick, sing about Hermes flying down to the ground!"

"But I—" Apollo started to protest.

"Just do it!" Athena yelled, her gray eyes flashing.

Apollo obeyed. *"Hermes flew back to the ground, he landed slowly without a sound."*

As he sang, Hermes slowly descended from the sky. He landed on two feet.

"What just happened?" he asked.

"It's the lyre," Athena began. "I think it's—"

But Apollo was singing again.

"I've never seen a monster like that, with the body of a horse and the head of a cat."

"Apollo, no!" Athena screamed.

Poof! The Leucrocotta appeared on the path in front of them. It looked confused for a second, and then its eyes narrowed when it saw the Olympians.

"It's back!" Aphrodite shrieked.

Ares shook his fist at the beast. "Back off, ugly! You won't trap us again!"

Zeus reached for Bolt again. "Where did that come from?"

Athena turned to Apollo. "I think your songs are making things real," she told him. "Sing the monster away! Quick!"

The Leucrocotta jumped toward the Olympians, his hooves kicking up dust in the path. Apollo started to sing as fast as he could:

"The monster's teeth began to gnash, and then it vanished in a flash!"

Poof! The Leucrocotta disappeared once more.

Apollo's hands were shaking on the strings. He turned to Hermes.

"What kind of lyre is this?" he asked, staring at his instrument.

Hermes shrugged. "I'm not sure. I just fixed it."

"I'll tell you what it is," Hera said. "Apollo, you have finally got your magical object!"

CHAPTER FOUR

Dionysus and the Goat Guys

Apollo stared down at the golden lyre.

"That is awesome, dude!" said Poseidon. "So why don't you look happy?"

"Because it's really different now," Apollo said. "I mean, I used to just make up silly songs as I went. Now I have to be really careful what I sing about."

"Well, maybe you could save the magic lyre

for when we're in trouble," Zeus suggested. "Like I do with Bolt."

Apollo nodded thoughtfully. "I guess so. I will miss strumming my lyre all the time, though."

"Then just get another wood one like the old one," Aphrodite said.

Apollo looked around. "We're in the middle of nowhere. Who even knows if the next village will have a lyre maker?"

Aphrodite laughed, and more bubbles floated up around her. "You can make one yourself, silly! Just sing about it."

Apollo's eyes lit up. "I guess I could," he said. He closed his eyes for a minute. Then he strummed the golden lyre and began to sing. *"I wished for a lyre to use as a spare, and one wooden lyre appeared in the air!"*

Poof! A simple lyre made of wood appeared

in the air in front of Apollo. He reached out and took it.

"It's real," he said, his eyes filled with disbelief. "This gold lyre really is magic!"

"Do you think you could maybe sing about roast pork next?" Hades asked, rubbing his belly. "Or spiced apples and figs? I'm really hungry."

"I would be careful using that magic lyre if I were you," Demeter warned. "Maybe it's like my magic seeds. I can grow anything with them, but once they're gone, they're gone. I need to save them for important things."

"But none of our other items have run out of magic," Hades said. He put on his Helm of Darkness and disappeared. "See? Works every time!"

He took off the helmet and appeared again.

"You're right, but I think it's a good idea for

Apollo to be careful," Hera said. "I mean, being able to make things real just by singing about them is pretty powerful!"

"I'll be careful," Apollo promised. "I don't want to magic up another monster again, that's for sure!"

Hades frowned. "So no roast pork?"

"We have plenty of food in our packs," Demeter said. She handed him a chunk of bread. "Here you go."

Hades bit into it. "Stale and crunchy. Just how I like it!"

"Now that we've got the whole lyre thing figured out, we should keep walking," Zeus said. "We need to get to the Land of Grapes!"

They walked for hours, taking only a few short breaks. They ate a little and refilled their water jugs from a bubbling stream. Because it was summer, they walked far before the sun started to sink in the sky, and they made camp. Hestia made a roaring campfire and they sat around it, tired and yawning.

Zeus glanced around the campsite. "I hope this fire doesn't attract any Cronies."

The half-giant warriors were loyal to King Cronus. They had been chasing the Olympians over land and sea ever since Zeus's journey had begun.

"You know, it's funny," Hera remarked. "Usually by now we'd be running or hiding from Cronies. But we haven't seen them for a few days.

"Maybe they've given up looking for us," Poseidon said hopefully.

"I don't think so," Zeus said. "Those Cronies might not be smart, but they're strong and they do whatever King Cronus tells them to do. And he wants them to capture us!"

The Olympians were quiet, thinking about this. Then Hera piped up.

"If Pythia is right, then we won't be running from the Cronies for much longer," she said. "We just need to find this last Olympian, battle King Cronus and his armies, and take our place as rulers of Greece."

"It's the whole 'battle King Cronus and his armies' part that's not so easy," Poseidon pointed out.

Ares jumped up. "Well, I'm not scared!" he yelled, his red eyes blazing.

Zeus yawned. "First, we have to find the last Olympian. Let's get some rest."

They slept through the night and headed out again early in the morning. Apollo was playing his not-magical lyre.

"Who will the last Olympian be? A he or a she? As short as a log, or as tall as a tree?" he sang.

"Tall as a tree? That sounds more like a Titan than an Olympian," Hestia remarked.

They walked all morning, took a rest at noon, and then walked some more.

"Chip, how much farther?" Zeus asked.

Chip answered in its own special language, Chip Latin. It was kind of like Pig Latin, only you moved the first letter of each word to the end of the word and added "ip."

"E-bip ere-thip y-bip unset-sip," Chip replied.

"We'll be there by sunset," Zeus repeated. He looked up at the sun, which was still high in the sky. "That's a long way to go."

But Chip was right—the sun was just starting to set when the green fields they were walking through turned into rows and rows of grapevines, growing on wood poles.

In the distance, Zeus could make out flickering torches. And a pulsing sound could be heard.

 41

"That sounds like drums," Poseidon remarked. "Do you think it's a Crony camp?"

Hermes flew ahead. "Let me check it out!"

He zipped forward on his winged sandals. The Olympians waited a few minutes until he came back.

"No Cronies," he reported. "It's some kind of festival! There are some guys drumming and another guy singing."

"Is there food?" Hades asked.

Hermes nodded. "Yup. Someone is selling pork kebobs."

"What are we waiting for, then?" Hades asked, and he darted forward.

The Olympians were all exhausted, but the prospect of music and food propelled them ahead. When they reached the festival, they saw a big crowd of people, young and old, dancing around a wood platform.

On top of the platform, a kid was singing. He wore a purple tunic and green pants. A ring of ivy crowned the top of his head, and golden-brown hair hung down his back. Behind him, four men with goat horns and hairy goat legs were banging on drums.

"Ooh ooh, ooh, feel the beat," the kid sang.

"Who are those guys?" Zeus wondered out loud.

"And what kind of song is that?" Apollo asked. "It doesn't even rhyme!"

One of the villagers, a young woman, spun around. "It's Dion and the Goat Guys! Haven't you heard of them? They're the best!"

She danced away from them.

"Those Goat Guys sure look like monsters," Athena remarked.

"Maybe, but they've got great moves," Poseidon said. He started dancing.

Aphrodite started to twirl. "This is fun!" she exclaimed. She grabbed Hestia with one hand and Demeter with the other, and pulled them into the dance.

"Wait!" Zeus called out. "We don't know who these guys are! They could be dangerous!"

Ares started jumping up and down and thrashing his head from side to side. "Maybe, but I don't care! This is awesome!"

Hephaestus tapped the ground with his cane and bopped his head. "Yeah, there's something really catchy about it. Makes you want to dance."

Hermes somersaulted in the air. "Definitely!"

Hera, Poseidon. Hades, Apollo, and Artemis joined the dance, twirling, jumping, and bopping along to the music. Zeus turned to Athena.

"I don't get it. What's happening?" he asked.

Athena shrugged. "I'm not sure, it's just—hey!"

She looked down at her feet. They were moving to the beat of the music!

"I'm not doing that!" she said. "It's like the music is . . . controlling us."

"Maybe you, but not me!" Zeus declared.

"Oh no?" Athena asked. She pointed down to Zeus's feet.

Zeus looked down. His feet were moving too! He couldn't stop them!

CHAPTER FIVE

No Autographs!

We need to stop whatever that guy is doing," Zeus cried, as he helplessly jumped around.

"How can we stop him when we can't stop dancing?" Athena shot back.

"We don't have to," Zeus said. He motioned to the other Olympians. "Come on, let's get closer to the stage!"

The others didn't stop dancing, but they

pushed through the crowd. Aphrodite, Hestia, and Demeter twirled and twirled, and Zeus wondered how they weren't dizzy. Ares kept bopping up and down. Poseidon and Hades kept bumping into each other and giggling.

Finally, they reached the stage. The boy, Dion, was still singing the same song.

"Ooh, ooh, ooh! Feel the beat!" he crooned.

Behind him, the Goat Guys were swaying to the beat as they drummed away.

"They definitely look like half-goat, half-human monsters," Athena told Zeus.

"But what about the kid? He looks normal," Zeus pointed out.

"I guess," Athena said. "But what's with the ivy crown?"

Hera danced up to them.

"Haven't you guys figured it out?" she

asked them. "This Dion kid must be the final Olympian!"

Zeus and Athena looked at each other in surprise.

"It makes sense," Hera continued. "He's our age. He's here in the Land of Grapes. And he seems to have some kind of weird power, because I can't stop dancing!"

"Of course!" Athena cried.

Hera grinned. "You're not the only clever one around here, you know!"

Suddenly, the drumming stopped.

"We're going to take a break!" Dion called out. "Everybody enjoy some delicious grape juice! We'll be back in a few minutes."

The Goat Guys stood up and stretched. Dion hopped off the platform, and Zeus tugged on Dion's sleeve.

"Excuse me, can I talk to you, please?" he asked.

Dion smiled. "Sorry, no autographs. They make my hand cramp up."

Hera rolled her eyes. "We don't want your autograph," she snapped. "We need to ask you some questions. We think you're an Olympian."

"An Olympian? Like, a god?" he asked. Then he smiled. "I wouldn't be surprised—I am pretty great onstage," he boasted. He held out his hand. "I'm Dion."

Hera shook it. "And I'm Hera, and this is Zeus, and Athena," she said. "So what exactly makes you think you're an Olympian? Being great onstage doesn't make you a god."

"Well, besides my awesome talents I've got magic powers," he said. "Don't all Olympians have magic powers?"

Zeus realized that some people in the crowd were listening to the conversation.

"Olympians?" a girl piped up. "Like the Olympians who are going to save us from King Cronus?"

Hephaestus responded to the girl. "That's right! Me and my friends here, we're Olympians!" he boasted.

Zeus nudged Hephaestus. "What are you doing?" he whispered. "I don't know if it's a good idea for everyone to know what we are!"

But it was too late.

"Really? Olympians?" someone else called out.

Hera shot Hephaestus an annoyed look.

More people started to crowd around Zeus and the Olympians. Dion frowned.

"So you guys are Olympians, for real? You don't look very awesome or magical," he commented. He nodded at Aphrodite, who was still spinning. Bubbles were floating all around her. "Except maybe for her, I guess."

The crowd was starting to ask questions.

"Did you really battle the Titans?"

"How are you going to defeat King Cronus?"

"Is it true that you can make lightning and thunder?"

Zeus was annoyed. They really needed to talk to Dionysus about joining them. They had traveled all this way to find him.

Two girls pushed between Zeus and Dion.

"Are you Zeus? Can we have your autograph?" one asked.

"Now, now," Zeus snapped. "Dion, we need to—"

But he couldn't see Dion. Then he heard a buzzing sound in his ear, like a bee.

And then, suddenly, he was standing in the middle of a bunch of grapevines. Other Olympians were standing around him, looking confused.

Zeus turned around. The stage wasn't even in sight.

Out of nowhere, Hades reappeared.

"Bro! Where did you go?" Zeus exclaimed.

Hades held his helmet under his arm.

"Well, that was weird. You won't believe what I saw!" he declared.

CHAPTER SIX

What a Jerk!

hat did you see?" Zeus asked.

"It was so weird!" Hades exclaimed.

"You already said that," Hera said impatiently. "Can you be more specific?"

"I got nervous when all those people started crowding around us," Hades explained. "So I put on my Helm of Darkness and became invisible."

"Nice trick, Bro!" Poseidon said.

Hades nodded. "When I'm wearing the helmet, it's hard to hear things. But I saw that Dion kid get kind of an upset look on his face. Then he opened his mouth, and I think he was singing."

"I don't remember that," Zeus said.

"Well, here's the thing," Hades continued. "You got weird all of a sudden."

"All of a sudden? Isn't Ares always weird?" Hephaestus joked, and Ares punched him in the arm.

"Hey!" Hephaestus protested.

"Not weird like Ares, I mean weird, like, your eyes all got blank. Then you all started walking into the grape fields. And you just kept walking and walking until you just stopped."

Athena frowned. "Maybe . . . maybe his song made us do it?"

Zeus nodded. "That's what I'm thinking.

Maybe when he sings, he can get people to do what he wants."

"That could be the awesome magical power he was talking about," Hera guessed. "And I bet that crown of ivy he wears is his magical object!"

"Then that dude is definitely the final Olympian!" Poseidon cried. "Come on, Bro, we've got to go get him."

"Hold up!" Zeus said. "We're not going anywhere near that guy right now. He could sing again and make us go away again."

"Or make us do something dumb, like pretend to be monkeys," Hades added.

Hera shook her head. "Why would he make us act like monkeys?"

"That's what I would do if I could control people," Hades replied. "It would be fun."

"Well, he's not going to get a chance to make us act like monkeys, or bunnies, or whatever, because we're going to come up with a plan," Zeus said. "A plan to make sure he can't use his magic on us again."

"He thinks he's awesome, but he's so annoying!" Hephaestus complained. "We should just leave him here."

"We can't do that," Zeus said. "Pythia said we needed to find the last Olympian before we could defeat King Cronus."

Hephaestus shrugged. "There are thirteen of us," he said. "That should be enough."

Hermes flew over to Hephaestus and landed next to him. "You guys thought I was an annoying jerk at first, and now you think I'm awesome, don't you?"

Hephaestus answered slowly. "Well . . ."

"Come on, Heff! Everyone thought you were a jerk too, when we first met you, but now we all know that you're not so bad," said Poseidon.

"No, he's still a jerk!" Ares said, and Hephaestus punched his arm this time.

"Notice how none of us girls are jerks," Hera said proudly.

"And anyway, each of us has our own special talent and magic," Demeter pointed out. "So we probably can't defeat King Cronus without Dion and his powers."

"Demeter is right," Zeus said. "Now, we just need a plan to make sure he doesn't use his powers on us again."

Hermes grinned. "Don't worry about that. I'll take care of it."

By now, Zeus knew that Hermes could do just about anything.

"Fine," Zeus said, nodding. "Then let's—"

"Danger!"

The Olympians looked up in surprise. A white cloud of mist suddenly appeared in front of the

Olympians. As the mist thinned, a woman in a white robe appeared. She had long black hair and wore fogged-up eyeglasses.

"Pythia!" Zeus yelled. "What are you doing here?"

"I'm here to warn you!" she said. "Danger is coming!"

"What kind of danger?" Zeus asked. "Is it the big monster you told us about last time?"

Pythia shook her head. "The monster waits, but there is a greater danger first. Now that there are fourteen Olympians, you must—"

"Um, we don't exactly have the fourteenth one yet," Zeus interrupted her. "I mean, we met him, but he doesn't seem to like us."

"You *must* get him to join you!" Pythia wailed. "A great danger is coming! It will be here soon."

"What kind of danger?" Hera asked.

"A great wave will rise up and swallow you," Pythia answered.

"You mean Oceanus?" Poseidon asked. They had battled the great Titan before. "But we're nowhere near the ocean."

"Not Oceanus," Pythia said. "Not a wave of water. A wave of—"

The mist began to shimmer and fade.

"A wave of what?" Zeus asked.

Pythia disappeared before she could answer.

"Well, that's just great, Boltbrain!" Hera yelled. "You let Pythia get away and we don't know what the danger is!"

"That doesn't matter right now," Zeus said. "We have to get Dion to join us, or we're all doomed! Come on, everybody!"

He raced back toward the festival stage, and the other Olympians followed him.

CHAPTER SEVEN

A Leader Rises

Zeus found Dion sitting on the edge of the stage, talking with his fans. Dion was eating up the attention, and didn't notice Hermes hovering above his head. With a quick swoop, Hermes flew down and took off with Dion's ivy crown.

"Hey, give that back!" Dion cried, jumping up.

"Not until we talk to you," Zeus said, his voice firm.

"Fine," Dion huffed, and he waved away the fans. "What do you want?"

"We need you to join us," Zeus replied. "You're one of us. And we need your help to fight King Cronus."

Dion shook his head. "Why would I want to do that?" he asked. "I've got a sweet gig, touring the countryside with the Goat Guys. I'm the star of this group. Why would I want to share the spotlight with you guys? And fight, besides! I'm a singer, not a fighter."

Hera stepped up. "But your crown gives you magic powers. You could help us with those."

"Isn't saving the land from King Cronus more important than singing?" Demeter added.

"Ha! Maybe for you," Dion said. "But I've got fans who count on me. Now, I've talked to you, like you wanted. Please, give me back my crown and let me finish my set."

"Fine, if you want your fans to think you're a coward," Zeus said darkly. He had to find some way to get through to this kid.

Dion looked Zeus right in the eyes. "My fans will think whatever I want them to," he replied.

Zeus looked up at Hermes and nodded. Hermes dropped the crown back on Dion's head.

Hera turned to him. "You heard Pythia, Boltbrain! We need this kid, even if he is an obnoxious side-show performer."

"I am *not* a side-show performer," Dion protested. "I'm the lead singer of a popular band."

At that moment, the ground underneath their feet began to rumble.

"Flipping fish sticks! What's happening?" Poseidon yelled.

"Is it an earthquake?" Hephaestus asked.

Hera's blue eyes grew wide. "This is no earthquake."

Zeus followed her gaze. Rows and rows of half-giant Cronies had appeared on the horizon in all directions. The loincloth-wearing, weapons-carrying soldiers of King Cronus trampled the grapevines as they stormed across the vineyard. Zeus had never seen so many Cronies in one place—and they surrounded the stage and the festivalgoers on every side. There was nowhere to run.

This was the danger Pythia had warned them about. Danger like a wave that would swallow them up. But this was no wave of water—it was a wave of Cronies!

"What now, Boltbrain?" Hera asked, and even though she was insulting Zeus, she sounded scared.

Zeus stood, frozen, not sure of what to do.

Boltbrain. Boltbrain. The words echoed in Zeus's head, and then it felt like a jolt of electricity shot through his brain.

Something kicked in—something deep inside him. His eyes scanned the battlefield. All the Olympians and their powers flashed through his mind.

He knew what to do, but they didn't have much time.

"Demeter, use one of your seeds! Grow something to protect the people! Hades, Aphrodite, help her!" he barked.

The three Olympians ran off without questioning him.

"Everyone else, on the stage!" Zeus commanded. "Apollo and Artemis, take the south side! Poseidon and Hestia, take the west! Ares,

Hephaestus, take the east! Athena, Hera, take the north with me! Hermes, take to the sky! But first, let's charge up!"

The Cronies shouted and whooped as they got closer to the stage.

"Bolt, large!" he cried, and his magical weapon sprang to life in his hand. He held it up in the air.

"Come on, everyone, hurry!" he yelled. Everyone held up their magical items: Athena's thread, Hermes's wand, Hera's peacock feather, Hestia's torch, Poseidon's trident, Ares's spear, and Hephaestus's cane. Apollo and Artemis were both gearing up their magical items, too—Apollo, his lyre and Artemis, her gold bow and silver arrows.

The weapons began to sizzle with energy as power surged through each one of them. The Olympians had learned this trick early on:

When they combined their items, each one became supercharged for a short time.

While the ten Olympians charged their weapons, Demeter, Hades, and Aphrodite tried to gather the frightened festivalgoers together.

Aphrodite seemed to have a calming effect on them.

"Come, take my hand," she said to a young girl, and the girl obeyed. One by one, Aphrodite brought the panicked crowd together, and Hades tried to help her gather them into a group.

Demeter took one magic seed out of the pouch she wore on her belt. She tossed it on the ground.

"Circle of thorns!" she yelled.

The seed immediately sprang to life. Thick stems quickly grew and twisted together, forming a circle around Demeter, Aphrodite, Hades, and the festivalgoers. Sharp thorns spiked out from the stems. The thorny wall grew twice as tall as the tops of their heads.

Back on the stage, the Olympians took their places as Zeus had ordered, facing the Cronies coming at them from four directions. Dion and his Goat Guys stood in the center of the stage, looking bewildered.

Zeus felt power surge inside him, power like he'd never felt before. Bolt sizzled in his hand. He stared out at the army of Cronies as the hulking, muscled brutes came closer.

They'd fought the Cronies before, small groups of them. Mostly, they had run away or hidden from the soldiers. But there was no running or hiding now. This time, they had to fight.

And win.

CHAPTER EIGHT

The Power of Thirteen

he Cronies charged forward, their voices sounding like thunder as they erupted in a battle cry.

Zeus turned to Hera. "Use your peacock feather to find out if more are coming. And if they've got any monsters with them."

Hera nodded and spoke to the feather, which was glowing with extra energy. She had

to speak in rhyme—or close to it—to get the feather to work.

"Feather, what I need to see is the number of this army, and if they are all Cronies."

The feather zipped off faster than a hawk, thanks to the extra Olympian power it held. Zeus turned to Athena.

"Any chance you'll use the aegis to turn these guys into stone?" he asked.

Athena had faced Cronies before, but refused to use the aegis against them. Now she looked out at the advancing army, her face tight with worry.

"I'd rather not," she replied. "They're still half-human, and being turned to stone is a horrible fate—even for a Crony."

Zeus nodded. "Use your thread then. Be clever."

Athena's gray eyes sparkled. "I can do that."

Zip. The feather flew back into Hera's hands.

She looked into its eye. Images of the Crony army appeared.

"Six hundred, I think, maybe more," Hera reported. "I don't see any Titans or monsters. Just Cronies."

"*Just* six hundred Cronies," Zeus repeated. "Great, no problem at all."

Six hundred Cronies against thirteen Olympians. It seemed impossible. But the Olympians had their magical weapons—and one another.

The Cronies were close enough to attack.

"Ooh, look at all those tasty Olympians," one of them yelled.

"It's time for dinner!" another added.

Zeus held up Bolt and was about to charge forward. To his surprise, Dion pushed past him.

"Let me show you how it's done," he said, and then he began to sing.

"Ooh ooh, Cronies, get off our back. Turn around, go home, and don't come back!"

Would it actually work? Zeus wondered. How awesome would that be if Dion's powers worked just as well on the advancing Cronies? One song from Dion and this whole thing could be over. . . .

But the Cronies kept charging.

Dion looked shocked. He stopped singing and took a step back as they pushed toward the group, totally not affected by the song.

"Do you have grapes for brains?" Hera snapped at Dion. "The Cronies can't hear your song. They're all yelling too loud!"

The Cronies were close enough that Zeus could see the sweat on their skin. Some had bushy beards. Others had shiny bald heads. Many had swirly designs tattooed on their bodies. They carried spiked clubs, axes, and spears and wore chest armor made of battered metal.

"Olympians, hold them back!" Zeus commanded.

Zap! He pointed Bolt at the Cronies closest to the stage. Three Cronies dropped, stunned by Bolt's power.

Three down, 597 to go, Zeus thought.

Hermes flew over the horde of Crony soldiers. He pointed his wand at a Crony.

"Freeze!" he commanded, and the Crony instantly stopped moving. Hermes grinned.

"It worked!" he announced, pleased with himself. He pointed his wand at another Crony. "Freeze!"

Next to Zeus, Athena was waving the Thread of Cleverness like a whip. The thread was so thin it was practically invisible, but it was stronger than the strongest metal.

"Hiyaaaaaa!" she yelled, wrapping the thread around a Crony right in front of her.

Thud! The thread brought the Crony to his knees.

"Hera, I need updates from your feather!" Zeus yelled, as he zapped another Crony.

"Feather, hurry, please don't snooze. Fly around and bring me news!" Hera told her feather, and it zipped away again.

On the west-facing side of the stage, Poseidon and Hestia were keeping the Cronies at bay with their weapons. Powerful blasts of water shot from Poseidon's trident, knocking back a row of attackers six Cronies deep.

"It's bath time, boys!" Poseidon yelled as he blasted another line of Cronies.

Hestia used her torch carefully—if she wasn't

careful, she could set the whole vineyard on fire, and she knew it. She aimed the flame at the feet of the Cronies, one at a time. The half-giants jumped backward, squealing, as the flames licked at their sandaled feet.

On the south-facing side of the stage, Artemis shot her silver arrows into the crowd of charging Cronies.

Three arrows flew. *Bam! Bam! Bam!* Each arrow hit a chest plate on a Crony. The force knocked the three Cronies backward.

The arrows returned to Artemis, and she readied another round. Apollo strummed his magical lyre and sang.

"Artemis aimed, her arrows flew. With every shot, her aim was true."

Bam! Bam! Bam! With the extra help from her brother's song, each of Artemis's arrows hit its mark.

On the east-facing side of the stage, Ares's red eyes burned like flames. He hurled his spear into the crowd of Cronies approaching him.

"Knock 'em down, spear!" Ares called out. "All Cronies shall bow at the feet of the mighty Ares!"

Bam! Bam! Bam! The spear knocked down three Cronies and then returned to Ares's hand.

Hephaestus looked at his cane. "All right, cane, I'm not really sure what you can do yet, but please do something to stop those Cronies!"

He threw the cane into the Cronies like Ares had thrown the spear.

Bam! Bam! Bam! The cane knocked down three Cronies, then flew back to Hephaestus.

"Nice!" he said, grinning. Then his eyes narrowed. "There's more where that came from, Cronies!"

Hera reported all this to Zeus when the feather returned to her.

"Good work!" Zeus called out. "Keep it up!"

Then behind him he heard a strange sound, like an animal cry. He looked behind him to see the four Goat Guys running toward him.

"Baaaaaaaaaaaa!"

They leaped off the stage and charged at the Cronies with their horns down. One by one, they rammed into them, pushing them back. They were helping the Olympians!

All around the stage, the Cronies were dropping. More Cronies came in behind them, but the Olympians—and their new goat friends—pushed them back.

We can do this, Zeus thought. *We can win!*

Then he heard the screams.

"Help! Help!"

He turned to see two dozen Cronies hacking

away at the fence of thorns that Demeter had grown with her magic seeds. The stems were as thick as the Cronies' arms, and hacking through them wasn't easy. But Zeus could see the stems beginning to break, and he knew it would be just a matter of time before the Cronies got through.

He threw Bolt at some of the Cronies hacking away at the thorns, zapping them. Bolt returned to his hand, but when he looked back to the attacking Cronies, he saw one had reached the stage and was about to grab his foot.

Zap! Zeus quickly blasted him back, but more were still coming. He couldn't help Athena defend the north side of the stage and help Demeter and the others at the same time. Maybe he could send someone. . . .

He took a quick look around. Poseidon's water blasts were putting out Hestia's fires, and the Cronies were quickly advancing on the east.

On the south, Artemis was hitting her targets, but there was only one of her, and she only had so many arrows. On the east side, he saw Ares's spear and Hephaestus's staff clash in midair. Those two still needed more practice with their weapons, he knew.

Zeus turned to Athena. "We're outnumbered," he said. "I don't think we can hold them off much longer."

Athena nodded. "I know."

"Think of something clever," Zeus said. "We need a really good idea to get us out of this."

"As powerful as our weapons are, there aren't enough of us to take down the Cronies," Athena said, whipping her Thread of Cleverness around a Crony as she spoke. "It's too bad Dion's song didn't work. We really just need the Cronies to turn around and go home."

Zeus glanced over at Dion, who stood in the

middle of the stage, looking defeated. His song would have worked, if only it could be heard. . . .

With perfect timing, Apollo began to strum his lyre and sing. *"Artemis shot her arrows faster and faster, saving the Olympians from disaster. . . ."*

The supercharged lyre was loud, Zeus realized. Loud enough to reach the first few rows of Cronies. . . .

He grinned at Athena. "I know what to do!"

CHAPTER NINE

Time to Face the Music!

Zeus zapped two more Cronies and then quickly turned to Dion. He was done asking for Dion's help. Now it was time to demand it.

"Dion, take off your crown and hold it above your head!" he yelled. His own voice surprised him. It sounded deep and commanding.

Dion obeyed without arguing. Zeus touched Bolt to the crown.

"Apollo, come here! We need your lyre!"

Apollo ran to join Zeus and Dion. He touched his lyre to the crown and Bolt. Energy surged through the objects, and a brilliant light exploded from them.

"Dion, put on the crown!" Zeus ordered. "I want you to sing. Apollo, you too. Make the Cronies turn around and walk back to Olympus. Tell them not to stop marching until they get there."

"I tried that, but they didn't hear me before," Dion protested.

"It will work this time," Zeus promised. "At least, I hope so!"

Apollo strummed his lyre. "You start, Dion," he said. "I'll join you."

Dion ran his fingers through his long hair. He started to sing.

"Cronies, do as I say. Turn around and go away."

His voice boomed out over the attacking Cronies this time, powered by the supercharged crown. The first five rows of attacking Cronies stopped suddenly. They all turned around and started to march away. But the rest of the Cronies kept coming.

"They're, like, fifty rows deep!" Hera yelled. "Dion needs to be louder!"

"I'm singing as loud as I can!" Dion protested, and his voice cracked as he spoke. "I'm going to lose my voice soon!"

"Keep singing!" Zeus ordered. "We'll figure something out."

"Cronies, march back to Olympus," Dion sang.

"The Cronies marched back to Olympus, and forgot they ever saw us," Apollo echoed.

The next row of Cronies turned back . . . but the others quickly rushed the stage. Zeus knew that Dion and Apollo would need to get much

87

louder, quickly, to defeat the whole army.

"I've got an idea!" Athena cried. She yelled up, "Hermes! Bring me one of Aphrodite's shells!"

Hermes nodded and flew inside the circle of thorns. He emerged a few seconds later carrying a cone-shaped seashell the size of his hand. He swooped down and handed it to Athena.

Athena placed the shell on the stage. She took her Thread of Cleverness and spelled out a word.

Louder

The shell began to grow larger and larger until it reached the size of a watermelon. Athena handed it to Dion.

"Sing through this!"

Dion held the thin end of the seashell to his lips. Then he sang through it.

"Cronies, march back to Olympus!"

Athena's invention amplified the magical sound. Zeus watched more Cronies turn and walk away. But Dion still couldn't reach all of them. If only he could fly above them . . .

"Hermes, can you give Dion a lift?" Zeus asked.

Hermes grabbed Dion under his arms and tried to lift him up. The wings on his sandals flapped furiously, but he only got an inch above the stage.

"Sorry, Zeus, I can fly, but I'm not that strong," Hermes said.

Zeus glanced over at the wall of thorns. The Cronies hacking away at the wall hadn't heard Dion's song.

"Keep singing!" Zeus told Dion and Apollo. Then he turned to Hermes. "Fly over to the wall and help the others. Freeze the Cronies, or try to get the axes away from them."

Hermes nodded. "You got it, boss!" And then he zipped away.

"Cronies, march back to Olympus. Keep marching until you get there." Dion sang.

Apollo sang the chorus. *"The Cronies marched back to Olympus. They forgot all about us."*

More Cronies turned away. But more kept coming. Ares and Hephaestus had control of their weapons again. Hestia switched places with Artemis, so her flames weren't getting doused by Poseidon's water blasts anymore.

Over at the wall of thorns, Hermes was zapping the axes out of the hands of the Cronies.

Zeus was proud of his team. They were working together and solving problems. But the wave of Cronies kept coming, just as Cronies were leaving, thanks to Dion and Apollo. It just wasn't enough.

"Something's coming!" Hera yelled.

She pointed up to the sky. A huge creature was flying across the vineyard. A white horse with wings. Riding on top of it was a boy with curly blond hair.

"It's Ron!" Zeus cried. "And Pegasus!"

Pegasus, the winged horse, had stolen Bolt not long ago. Zeus had tracked down the horse and found him with Ron, a kid with a big problem. His uncle needed him to take down a terrible monster, a chimera. The Olympians had helped Ron with his monster problem. Zeus got Bolt back, and Ron and Pegasus had stuck together.

Pegasus landed on the stage, his huge wings flapping.

"You guys need some help?" Ron asked with a big grin.

CHAPTER TEN

A Little Help from a Friend

Zeus didn't hesitate.

"Dion, Apollo, climb on the horse's back!" he yelled.

The two boys quickly obeyed. Pegasus was large enough to carry both of them and Ron, too.

"Ron, I need you to fly over all the Cronies," Zeus said. "Their song can drive the Cronies away."

"Got it!" Ron replied. "Come on, Pegasus!"

 93

The horse whinnied and lifted off into the sky. He slowly circled the vineyard as Dion and Apollo sang.

"Go away and don't come back!" Dion commanded them.

"The Cronies left and didn't come back!" Apollo sang.

From the sky, their sound reached far and wide. Each and every Crony heard the song. Dion's words sneaked into their minds, making them do what Dion said. Apollo's magical lyre made the whole plan real.

The Cronies marched away from the vineyard. They stomped over the grapevines. They trampled the dirt under their feet.

But they had stopped fighting.

"They're leaving!" Hera cheered.

There were no more Cronies around the wall of thorns. Before they left, they'd chopped a

hole big enough for humans to walk through. Demeter, Aphrodite, and Hades came through it, followed by Dion's festival fans.

Stomp! Stomp! Stomp!

The ground shook as the Cronies marched away. Soon the last one disappeared over the horizon.

The crowd let out a cheer. Pegasus landed back on the stage, and Dion, Ron, and Apollo climbed off his back. Dion and Apollo high-fived.

"We sounded great together!" Dion said. "We should team up more often."

"We should team up all the time," Apollo said.

"That's right," Zeus said. "You see what we're up against. We need you."

Dion looked thoughtful. "Can I bring my Goat Guys with me?" he asked.

"Of course you can," said Zeus.

"Oh great," Hera said, wrinkling her nose. "Have you smelled those guys? They smell like a wet barnyard."

"*Baaaaaa!*" the Goat Guys protested.

"They don't smell *that* bad," Hades argued. "And besides, we need all the help we can get."

"If they're in, I'm in," Dion said. "And Dion is just my stage name. My real name is Dionysus."

Demeter nodded. "Now, that sounds like an Olympian!"

Zeus turned to Ron. "How did you know we needed help?"

"Well, I was just hanging with Pegasus in the stable, when this mist appeared and . . ." Before Ron could finish his sentence, a cloud of mist appeared in front of the Olympians. The mist dissolved to reveal Pythia.

"Pythia, you're back!" Hera cried.

"I wanted to make sure that Ron got here in time to help you," she said.

Ron stepped forward. "I did!"

"Yeah, we sent those Cronies packing!" Ares chimed in.

"That's good," Pythia said. "And I see you've found the last Olympian. That's good, too, because you are about to face your biggest challenge yet."

"You said we would face our biggest monster," Zeus reminded her. "Can you tell us anything more?"

Pythia shook her head. "My spectacles are foggy. All I know is that the monster is big, and that it's dragging something."

"Dragging something?" Hades repeated.

Ron's eyes lit up. "Wait, I think I know!" he cried. "There are rumors in the kingdom that the Titans are gathering at Olympus. And they have an enormous *dragon*!"

"Ah yes, that's it," said Pythia. "A dragon. Of course."

"Do you know what kind of dragon, exactly?" Athena asked.

"I am afraid not," Pythia said. "Only that it will take all fourteen of you to defeat it and dethrone King Cronus. If you do not, something terrible will happen. The world will . . ."

The mist started to swirl around, and Pythia faded. Her final words were lost.

"Whoa. That was intense," Hades remarked.

"Well, I'm not afraid of any dragon!" Ares yelled. "I'll take him down with my spear!"

"And I'll attack him with my cane!" Hephaestus added.

Then the Olympians started talking all at once.

"We can do it!"

"What's a dragon? Just another monster!"

"Nothing can stop us!"

Zeus's thunder voice rose above the others.

"Then it's settled!" he said, and the others quieted down. The others were treating him like a real leader, he realized. He stood up a little straighter. "Tonight, we rest! Tomorrow, we march to Olympus to defeat King Cronus!"

The Olympians started to cheer, but Hera stopped them. "And the dragon. And maybe some Titans. And we just sent the Crony army there, Boltbrain, so we might have to face them again too."

Zeus sighed. He had a feeling that even if he did end up ruling Greece one day, Hera would still call him Boltbrain.

"It doesn't matter," Zeus said. "Because we are all together now. We are fourteen Olympians strong. Nothing can stop us!"

Looking for another great book?
Find it
IN THE MIDDLE.

Fun, fantastic books for kids
in the in-be**TWEEN** age.

IntheMiddleBooks.com

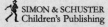

Join Zeus and his friends
as they set off on the
adventure of a lifetime.